A PRICKLY PROBLEM

CALPURNIA TATE ✧ GIRL VET

A PRICKLY PROBLEM

BY JACQUELINE KELLY

WITH ILLUSTRATIONS BY JENNIFER L. MEYER

GODWINBOOKS

HENRY HOLT AND COMPANY · NEW YORK

HENRY HOLT AND COMPANY, *Publishers since 1866*

Henry Holt® is a registered trademark of Macmillan Publishing Group, LLC
175 Fifth Avenue, New York, NY 10010 · mackids.com

Library of Congress Control Number: 2017945036

ISBN 978-1-62779-875-4

Our books may be purchased in bulk for promotional, educational,
or business use. Please contact your local bookseller or the Macmillan
Corporate and Premium Sales Department at (800) 221-7945 ext. 5442
or by e-mail at MacmillanSpecialMarkets@macmillan.com.

First edition, 2018 / Designed by April Ward and Carol Ly
Printed in the United States of America by LSC Communications, Harrisonburg, Virginia

1 3 5 7 9 10 8 6 4 2

For animal lovers everywhere

One thing I've learned is that some dogs are pretty smart, and some dogs are pretty dumb, and most of the time it's not too hard to tell the difference between them. (I've learned that people are like that too.) But with some dogs, well, you just never know what you're getting. I'm thinking here of Ajax, my father's prize bird dog. You'd think a dog that won prizes for hunting birds would have at least a little common sense, wouldn't you? You probably would. I know *I* sure did, until that dumb dog proved me wrong in a really big way. Let me tell you about it.

It was early autumn in 1901. The crushing summer heat had ended. All

around us were the welcome signs of animals getting ready for the coming winter: the cats' fur grew thick, the hummingbirds departed for the south, the Canada geese arrived from the north. The squirrels rushed around burying as many pecans as they could, patting the soil into place with their tiny paws like busy little gardeners.

My six brothers and I would be going back to school in another week. But before that, we always gave away our old clothes to the poor at the other end of town. Every year, Mother would put together a big wicker basket of boots and clothes, and we'd deliver it to the needy.

This time, Mother said, "Calpurnia, I notice that your bedroom is getting overrun with books. I think it's time to part with some of them, so pack a few in the hamper as well."

"*What?*" I was outraged.

"Watch your tone, young lady, and do as I say."

"You don't give away *books*," I said.

"Why on earth not?" She continued sorting and packing.

4

"Well, I . . . I don't know. It's just not right. Somehow." I sounded lame, even to myself.

"Hmm."

I trudged heavily up the stairs in a black mood. Give away my books? What a terrible idea. I finally picked out an old book that I had long outgrown: *A Child's Collection of Fairy Tales*. The cover was faded and the pages dog-eared. On the cover, a giant wielding a club and dressed in green chased after a small boy dressed in brown: "Jack and the Beanstalk." My three older brothers had read all those stories to me, and I in turn had read them to my three younger brothers. That book was part of my childhood. It didn't feel right, giving away part of my past. But the shelf was getting crowded, and the other books had to do with birds and mammals and plants and fossils—all part of my present. (And, I hoped, my future.) I couldn't give those away. I sighed and grabbed the fairy tales and ran downstairs. I comforted myself with the thought that I knew the tales so well that they were fixed forever on the bookshelves lined up in my brain. That is to say, in my memory.

This year we were visiting the Thompson family. We loaded the hamper onto my younger brothers' red wagon, and I pulled it down the street with Mother.

It was hard to tell exactly how many children the Thompsons had. Each time we visited, there seemed to be yet another grubby little face peering out from behind Mrs. Thompson's skirts. The youngest Thompsons went barefoot, even in winter; the older ones wore our cast-off boots. All but the very youngest had to help out on the farm from time to time, so they missed many days of class and lagged behind in school.

Mrs. Thompson's eyes lit up when she opened the door and saw the hamper in the wagon. Mother handed out the clothes to the children of various sizes. One of the younger girls eyed the fairy-tale book. I think her name was Milly, or maybe Molly.

I plucked it from the hamper and handed it to her. She took it with big round eyes, plunked herself down on the floor, and started paging through it right away. Mother and Mrs. Thompson chatted about this and that, and I heard Mother promise to bring a turkey at Thanksgiving. We always raised three: one for us, one for the help, and one for the poor.

When it was time for us to go, Milly (or maybe Molly) stood up and handed the book back to me. "That's all right," I said. "You can keep it."

"What?" she said, looking puzzled.

"You can keep it."

"You mean . . . you don't want it back?"

"No, it's your book now."

"My book?"

"Yes," I said.

"*My* book?"

"Yes," I said, thinking she must be a little slow or a little deaf.

Then she said something that made it all clear. "I've never had my own book before."

"Oh," I said, taken aback. "Well, uh, you do now."

She stammered her thanks and hugged it to her chest like a great treasure.

And here was I, Calpurnia Virginia Tate, with a dozen books on a shelf by my bed, and hundreds more in my grandfather's room, and thousands more at the Lockhart library. All the books I wanted, really. Was I not the luckiest girl in the whole world? Why, yes, I was. And was I not the most self-ish as well? Well, yes, that too. I told myself I would never complain about giving away a book again as long as I lived.

On our walk home, Mother shook her head, saying, "How that poor woman manages, I'll never know."

We walked on in silence until she said, "You're being very quiet today."

I said nothing because I had nothing to say.

Early Friday Travis and I went out for a walk to the riverbank. Ajax decided to trail along with us, bounding through the brush and sniffing everything in sight. Travis was telling me some boring story about something my friend Lula had done at school. I admit I wasn't paying much attention.

Up ahead, I caught sight of a strange fat little creature waddling along. It turned around to look at us. With its big front teeth and round body, it looked a lot like a beaver, except, of course, for all the fearsome quills sticking out.

Ajax, who'd been
busy sniffing around,
suddenly looked up and
caught sight of it. He bolted at
it, barking his head off at this
stranger on his turf.

"Ajax! Stop!" I screamed.

The porcupine ran to the
nearest tree and climbed up
it at a surprising speed.

Granddaddy and I had seen one at the riverbank a few weeks before, and I remembered him telling me they were good climbers. Slow on the ground but fast in the trees.

The porcupine looked down at us, chewing peacefully on a bit of bark. It was actually kind of cute, except for being covered in those terrible quills. We finally hauled Ajax away by his collar.

"Gosh," said Travis, "that was a close one."

"Yep, way too close for comfort."

The next day, it was time for a family trip to Sutherland's Emporium, the huge department store in Lockhart, where we'd buy school supplies and new boots and cloth for Mother to sew us our school clothes. I didn't care that much about the clothes, but it was important to Mother that all the Tate children looked "presentable."

The Emporium was huge, three stories tall, and the biggest, most exciting store for fifty miles around. Nobody in their right mind would miss a trip.

My six brothers and I crammed into the wagon with Alberto, the hired man, driving; Mother and Father and Granddaddy rode in the buggy. But before we left, we tied up poor Ajax on the porch so he wouldn't follow Father. He loved Father dearly and hated to be separated from him. He'd once followed us all the way to Lockhart and back and been a perfect nuisance the whole way, worrying livestock and barking at strangers on the road, and almost crushing his paws under the wagon wheels. We gave him a big bowl of water and patted him and told him to be a good boy. Even so, he fought the rope and barked like crazy until we were well out of sight.

Normally there might have been some elbowing and pinching and braid pulling on the trip but not today. We all knew that our good behavior would be rewarded with a sweet, gooey treat at the soda fountain, one of the high points of our lives!

I kept the younger boys entertained by pointing out the flora and fauna that I had learned about from Granddaddy. But the youngest, Jim Bowie, soon grew tired of this and started making animal noises whenever he spotted one. We saw lots of cows and horses and pigs on the way, so it got annoying pretty fast.

The Lockhart square was bustling with Saturday shoppers. We parked in front of the store and went in, all except for Granddaddy. He headed across the square to the library, carrying a long list of books he wanted to check out.

The minute you walked into the store, you could smell all the enticing smells from the soda fountain, the chocolate and the caramel and the crushed fruits in syrup. Yum! But first we had business to attend to.

"Now, come along, all of you," said Mother, "and don't scatter. First, the shoe department."

We lined up in the shoe department, and each got fitted with a handsome new pair of boots. Mine were chestnut leather, so shiny you could see your reflection in them. My old ones looked very scuffed and tired beside them.

Mother handed over money to the clerk, who put it into a metal capsule about the size of a hot dog bun. He then pushed it into a pneumatic tube, which whooshed away on a current of compressed air to the cashier in the basement. The cashier made change, which then whooshed back to us. A very interesting system. Granddaddy had told me there was some talk in the big cities of moving people from place to place the same way, only in bigger capsules, of course.

Then it was time to buy school supplies. I loved getting new yellow pencils, and a new pencil box to keep them in, and a fresh new copybook. No matter that the pencils would soon be covered in tooth marks since I tended to gnaw on them while thinking. No matter that the copybook pages would soon be crumpled and torn. It was the promise of a fresh start that counted.

Then Mother bought several bolts of fabric, and Alberto carried them out to the wagon. Father went off to the barbershop for a haircut and a hot shave, and to catch up on the latest news from Austin. And since we'd all been well behaved, Mother gave us money for the soda fountain while she went upstairs to the mezzanine for cream puffs and afternoon tea. The mezzanine was a kind of half floor sticking out over the ground floor where the ladies with their huge hats could look down on the action below. Mother couldn't hear us, but she could definitely still see us, so we had to behave. Sort of.

I loved sitting at the counter and watching the soda man perform his magic of pouring fizzy floats and building colorful sundaes. I chose a root beer float and drank it very, very slowly to make it last longer.

When we got home, we discovered that Ajax had somehow slipped out of his collar and disappeared. But since everyone in Fentress knew him, we figured some neighbor would bring him home or else he'd wander back in a few hours for dinner. He'd never been

known to miss a meal. Even Father didn't seem too worried about him.

And sure enough, while we were eating our own dinner, he did wander back. He made funny noises and scratched at the front door, which was unusual for him.

"That must be Ajax," Father said.

"I'll get him," Travis said, and ran from the table to let the dog in. Ajax was only allowed in the hallway, and only when he was clean and dry. He longed to worm his way deeper into the house, but it was absolutely forbidden.

Travis came back. He looked pale and kind of wobbly.

"What's the matter, dear?" said Mother.

"I don't feel so good." He plopped down in his chair.

"What's wrong?"

He pressed his napkin to his mouth and muttered something that sounded like *pork pie*.

Father shoved himself from the table and strode out into the hall, the rest of us—except for Travis and Mother—following on his heels.

Ajax sat in the hall whimpering, but it wasn't his usual noise. The strange sound was due to the fact that he didn't

want to open his mouth. And the rea-
son he didn't want to open his mouth
was because of the dozen quills stuck in
his muzzle.

"Oh no," said Father, "he's got a
porcupine."

I thought it looked more like a
porcupine had got him, but now was

not the time for smart remarks. Was it the same one Travis and I had seen? Not that it mattered.

Ajax shivered.

Granddaddy stepped forward and grabbed him tightly by the scruff, holding his head high.

"Quick, Alfred," he said to Father, "hold his front legs. Don't let him paw himself. He'll only push the quills deeper. Where is his collar? We need to restrain him."

My oldest brother, Harry, said, "I'll get it."

"I'll fetch Dr. Pritzker," I said, and

dashed out the front door at full speed before Father could appoint someone else to go.

Dr. Pritzker was the town's animal doctor. Sometimes he let me help him in his office. Sometimes, when no one else was around, he taught me about doctoring animals. It was our secret. Ladies weren't supposed to know about such things. (My mother was determined to make me a lady, an uphill battle if ever there was one.)

Dr. Pritzker's office was a ten-minute walk or a four-minute run from our house. I caught the doctor just as he was leaving for the night. I told him what had happened, and he said, "That's a shame. Your father's very fond of that dog. We've got to get the quills out before they migrate and pierce a vital organ. I've seen dogs die that way."

He fetched his bag, and we headed for our house. By the time we got there, they'd put a collar on Ajax and were holding him still. Father stroked the dog's flank and spoke soothing words to him so he wouldn't panic. Ajax rolled his eyes in pain.

"Ah," said Dr. Pritzker when he saw him. "It's not so bad. I've seen much worse, believe me, sometimes hundreds of quills, enough to kill a dog. We should have him fixed up in no time."

He pulled out what looked like a pair of pliers and said, "Hold him very still, now. The barbs work their way in deeper every time he moves." Father and Granddaddy held the dog. I thought there might be some special way of removing the quills, but no. Dr. Pritzker simply grabbed a quill with the pliers and pulled. Hard. It came out with a little *pop*. Ajax yelped, but Dr. Pritzker continued, working swiftly. A couple of minutes later, they were out. That's all there was to it.

Then he carefully felt Ajax's muzzle
to make sure there were none left bur-
ied under the skin. When he was satis-
fied, he stood up, saying, "Well, at least
he's learned his lesson. Keep an eye on
him for the next couple of days and let
me know if there are any problems."

Father looked relieved. "Will he be
fit for hunting season?"

"Yes, he'll be fine. And you won't
have to worry about him getting stuck
again."

Mother and Travis, who'd been in
the dining room all this time, finally
came out of hiding. Mother said, "Oh,

the poor dog. Thank you so much for coming, Dr. Pritzker."

Travis looked away. He'd always had a soft heart for animals. And a touchy stomach as well.

I went to bed that night figuring that Ajax and I had both learned something new about life. And porcupines.

4

And speaking of learning something new, it was time for school
to start. Our town had a one-room
schoolhouse with only one teacher,
Miss Harbottle, who taught all ages.
She and I were not exactly the best of
friends. She thought I was a "smartie"

who liked to show off the extra stuff I
learned outside of school. Living with
Granddaddy, of *course* I learned all
kinds of extra stuff. I couldn't help it.
You would too.

The classroom still smelled faintly
of skunk. Why, you may ask? Well,
Travis had brought his pet skunks to
school a few months earlier, with
predictable results. They'd been airing
out the school all summer, so at least it
was bearable.

There was a new boy none of us had
ever seen before, the nephew of Mr.
Chadwick, the owner of the general

store. The boy's name was Woodrow Chadwick, and he looked about my age.

Milly gave me a shy smile. (I'd checked on her name and found out she was Milly for sure, not Molly.) She was wearing my old boots and a patched hand-me-down dress. I was glad to see her. She'd be pulled out of school soon enough to help with the fall harvest, so she had to learn as much as she could, as fast as she could. And, unlike me, she didn't have a Granddaddy of her own to teach her about the world. Nobody did. I had the only one.

At recess, I went up to Woodrow in the far corner of the yard to introduce myself. I figured it was the neighborly thing to do.

To my amazement, he sneered at me. "So you're the famous Calpurnia Tate. I've heard all about you, and your weird grandfather."

I was shocked. He was shocked too, at finding himself flat on the ground exactly one second later. Somehow he had run straight into my fist. I looked around quickly. No one seemed to have noticed.

Being a good sport, I held out a hand

to help him up, but he swatted it away. He scrambled to his feet and stared at me with big eyes. "You're crazy!"

"If I am, I don't care," I said. "But don't you ever say anything about my grandfather ever again. He's the smartest man in all of Texas."

Woodrow ran off, and I rubbed my sore knuckles. Ouch. It had been worth it, but I still felt kind of bad.

After school let out, Milly sidled up to me and said, "Thank you for the book. I like it a lot, and my little brother does too. I read the stories to him because he doesn't know how to read yet. But now he wants to learn, just because of your book. I'm teaching him his ABCs."

"It's *your* book now, Milly." I decided it was time to part with some more books; it was time to help Milly Thompson fill her own shelf. It wouldn't kill me.

Then Milly whispered, "I'm glad you hit that boy. He's been mean to everybody all day."

"You saw that?" I was startled. "Was he mean to you too?"

She looked down at my—*her*—boots, which I could now see were much too big for her. She spoke so quietly I could barely hear her. "He said we were . . . poor people. And that he didn't talk to poor people." She flushed and looked close to tears. "But that's all right, 'cause I don't want to talk to him either."

Ugh, that horrible boy. I suddenly didn't feel bad about punching him. "Milly," I said, "if he's ever mean to you again, I want you to tell me, okay?"

"Okay."

"You promise?"

"I promise." She hesitated, then said, "I wish I was brave like you."

Brave? I'd never thought of myself as brave before, but it made me feel good. "Well, Milly, you're awfully young to be brave. How old are you?"

"I'm nine."

Truth be told, her skinny arms and legs and too-big clothes made her look even younger. I said, "Maybe you'll grow braver as you grow up."

"I hope so."

Travis and my friend Lula were waiting on me to walk home. Milly lived in the other direction or I would have invited her to join us. We said our good-byes and ran off.

That night, I picked out two more books for her. Then another three on top of that. Now that I knew Milly's circumstances, it wasn't painful to part with them. In fact, it made me feel kind of warm inside.

Over the next week, that pill Woodrow Chadwick started making friends with my older brother Lamar, who was kind of a pill in his own right. They deserved each other.

Whenever I ran into Woodrow on the playground, which wasn't often since he kept his distance, I'd say, "Why, hello, Woodrow." I'd smile and say it just as nice as pie. I could tell it made him nervous. He shied away every time like a spooked horse. He thought I was up to something, but I really wasn't (unless you count making him nervous, of course).

What with school and the shorter hours of daylight, I got to spend less time outdoors with Granddaddy. But after homework and dinner, I could sometimes grab a spare half hour with him in the library, and we would sit reading by lamplight and talking about dinosaurs and fossils. I'd become very interested in them since digging up my own ammonite; although it had been dead for millions of years, it now "lived" on top of my dresser.

Then it was hunting season. Father spent all his free time out hunting, crouched in a blind, sometimes with friends, always with Ajax. It was the dog's job to race across the field and fetch the dead birds that had fallen to earth.

He was good at his job, and he clearly loved it. Sometimes the bird came down on the other side of the river and he had to cross it with the bird in his mouth. That part was hard work. It's lucky he was such a big dog and a strong swimmer. I'd once seen him dive into the river and come back with two birds in his mouth *at the same time*. Of course, they weren't the huge Canada geese—no dog in the world could manage that—but still, it was quite a feat. Father turned down shockingly large sums of money for him every year. I had no idea a dog could be worth so much.

We had goose or dove nearly every night for dinner. That is, all of us except Travis, who just couldn't bring himself to eat an animal. He especially had trouble when we had venison, which is just a fancy word for dead deer. Mother and Father had long given up on trying to make him eat it, since it would likely come right back up, like an owl horking up its pellet. And who wanted to see *that* at the table?

On Saturday, I crept downstairs and slipped out before sunrise. The house was still asleep, but Ajax was awake on the front porch. He greeted me with his usual joy. One of the nice things about dogs is that you can be gone for a few hours, and then, when you come back, they act like they'd given up all hope of ever seeing you again.

I patted him and said, "All right, I guess you can come along. But you have to be quiet."

Ha. Fat chance of that. He crashed through the underbrush ahead of me, ears flopping, tongue lolling, tail wagging.

"Ajax, you may be a very good hunting dog, but you're a very bad Science dog. You've scared every living thing away."

But this wasn't true.

We came into a clearing, and there, on the other side, was a porcupine. On the ground. Where it did not belong. Oh no. Why wasn't it in a tree? Ajax was too busy sniffing to catch sight of it. Yet.

"Here, boy." I whistled softly to the dog.

The porcupine turned at my whistle and rustled in the leaves. Ajax looked up and saw it. For just one second, time slowed . . . way down . . . and then seemed to . . . stop. I held my breath. I looked at the dog. The dog looked at the porcupine. The porcupine looked at

me. For just one second, we stood fixed in place like that, a triangle of doom. I thought, *Please don't, please don't.* And then I thought, *Don't be stupid, don't be stupid.*

So. Let us take a step back from this scene of possible tragedy for a moment. Do you remember me telling you that there are smart dogs and dumb dogs in this world? And that it's usually easy to tell the difference? Here's how you tell. Smart dogs learn from their mistakes. Dumb dogs don't. That's the definition of being smart, you see, learning from your mistakes. So guess what? We owned the dumbest dog of all.

He growled deep in his chest, a scary rumble that made the hairs on the back of my neck stand up. I'd never heard such a frightening sound come from him. In front of my eyes, our playful family dog had become a wild animal.

Ajax charged. I screamed, "Nooooo!" He veered off right before running into the porcupine. It hunkered down to protect its belly. Ajax barked at it in a frenzy. I couldn't believe it. After what he'd been through, you'd think he'd run the other way as fast as he could.

"Stop it!" I screamed. "You come here right now."

He ignored me. The porcupine lashed its tail from side to side. I ran up and tried to grab Ajax by his collar, but he jumped away from me. He faked another lunge, and another, barking and growling, leaping back and forth, just out of range. The porcupine chittered in distress and swung its tail around. It puffed up its quills so they stood on end like a cat's fur. But deadly.

The porcupine slowly backed up to a tree. If I could only distract Ajax, if I could only give the porcupine a moment, it would escape up the tree. We'd all be home free.

But it was not to be.

The dog lunged at the same time the porcupine lashed. Ajax screamed in agony and staggered back. The porcupine hauled itself up the tree and disappeared.

I stared at Ajax in shock. The poor dog! His muzzle, face, and ears were covered with hundreds of quills, more than I could possibly count. I'd never seen such a horrible sight. He drooled and panted and made a soft grunting sound with each breath. What really scared me most was that this dog, who'd never stood still in his life, now stood very still, as still as a statue. His eyes were squeezed to slits. The slightest movement must have been agony.

I looked around and screamed, "Help! Anybody there? Please, I need help!"

There was no sound but the wind in the trees.

Think, Calpurnia, think. Should I leave him and run for help? But he might paw himself. He might wander off to die alone. I knew that dogs did that. We might not find him in time. Should I try to pull the quills out? I shuddered at the thought. And, besides, what would I use? I had no tools. If I used my hands, I'd end up with the quills in me.

I should take him to Dr. Pritzker, if I could only figure out how. I had no leash, no rope. I had nothing. Think,

Calpurnia, think. Granddaddy had taught me to look at the world in new ways through new eyes. He'd also taught me to "improvise" if what you needed wasn't at hand. I looked around the clearing and saw only trees and downed branches and old leaves. Not much help there. I looked down at myself. I had nothing except a pinafore and my dress, and my Scientific Notebook and pencil, and my new boots. With laces. Bootlaces. Hmm, if you thought about it, I was wearing a leash, sort of. I sat down and unlaced my boots and ended up with almost four feet of "rope."

I had to tie the laces together with a square knot that would hold tight, not a granny knot that would come apart under pressure. They looked very similar, but there was some little tip that explained the square knot. How did it go again? Ah, yes, "right over left, left over right." I made the knot, tested it, and then I very carefully slid one end of the new leash under Ajax's collar. He stood perfectly still and grunted. Somehow, this scared me more than him thrashing around and yelping. And even though I was very, very careful, and even though he moved not a muscle, I managed to stick myself with one of the quills. It hurt, unbelievably. It was astounding that just one quill could cause so much pain. I tried very hard not to think about what hundreds of them in my face would feel like. I made another square knot in the ends of the new leash.

"Ajax," I said, "I know you're hurt. We're going to get you help. I know you don't want to move, but you have to. That's all there is to it."

I tugged gently on the leash. He didn't move.

"Come, Ajax, come."

I patted my leg and gave the command again. He didn't move. I was afraid to pull too hard in case my knots came apart.

I squatted down in front of him and stared into his slitted eyes to show him who was in charge. "Ajax," I said sternly, "you have to come with me. It's for your own good, and that's all there is to it."

I stood up, patted my leg, and pulled hard on the leash, saying *"Come"* in a very serious tone of voice.

He took one stiff step forward. Then another. I kept up the pressure on his leash. And slowly, ever so slowly, we made our way along the trail. My boots were loose on my feet, but they stayed on. I made encouraging noises to Ajax as long as he kept moving, and spoke to him very strictly if he looked like he was going to stop. So, cajoling one moment and commanding the next, we made it to the road. I guess it took about half an hour, but it felt like a lifetime.

Fortunately, we'd come out on the road not far from my father's cotton gin, close enough for me to feel safe making a run for it. The street was clear of horses and carts, so I dropped the leash, and told him to "*Stay!*" on the edge of the road, and ran for the gin. One of my boots came off as I ran, and I almost fell flat in the dirt.

The old codgers in the rocking chairs in front of the gin watched me hobble up at a half run.

"Hey there, missy, thrown a shoe, I see. Heh heh."

"Better get you to the blacksmith. Ha ha."

I ignored them and rushed into Father's office. He looked up. I panted, "Ajax . . . porcupine."

"That's ridiculous, not again. Well, I suppose we'll just have to call Dr. Pritzker." He was still sitting at his desk, and he didn't seem particularly alarmed. I realized he was thinking that this episode was a repeat of the first one.

I said, "Bad . . . this time. . . . Hurry."

He got up, and we rushed out together, me limping along as best I could. Ajax hadn't moved a muscle. My strong stalwart Father grew pale when he saw his dog. By now, Ajax's muzzle was so swollen he looked like a monster in a fairy tale. Most pitiful of all, he feebly wagged his tail—just once—when he saw my father.

Without a word, Father very gently scooped up the dog in his arms and turned for Dr. Pritzker's office. Ajax must have weighed a good sixty pounds, but my father carried him as if he were no weight at all, walking as fast as he could, trying not to jar him. I kicked off my other boot and ran ahead in my stocking feet to the doctor's place.

I got there a minute or two before Father. A note on the door said, *Gone to Prairie Lea Farms, back at 5:00 p.m.* Oh no. It was only noon.

I knew that Dr. Pritzker left his door unlocked, and I opened it for Father. He came in and stood Ajax on the exam table. The dog's legs wobbled, but he kept to his feet. How long before he collapsed?

"Fetch the doctor," Father said.

"He's in Prairie Lea," I said, showing him the note.

Father groaned. "I'll have to borrow a horse from the blacksmith and ride for him." He looked at me as if suddenly realizing that I was only a child. "Can you . . . stay with him? Can you do that?"

"Of course I can," I said stoutly.

"Good girl. That's good. I'll be back as fast as I can."

He ran out the door and around the corner to the blacksmith. I looked at Ajax. Ajax looked at me. There was now pink-tinged foam dripping from his jaws. That couldn't be good. And I swear that some of the quills near his eyes looked . . . shorter. Which meant that they were moving. Inward.

Here's what went through my head: Prairie Lea is seven miles away. It will be at least two hours until they get back. Ajax is suffering. Maybe he'll go blind. Maybe he'll die. Don't just stand there; *do* something.

Right.

I've discovered that making up your mind to do something is often the hardest part of actually doing something, harder than the actual doing itself. I went to the drawer where I knew Dr. Pritzker kept his equipment, and found a thing that looked like the pliers he'd used before. I turned to Ajax and took a deep breath. "I hope you'll forgive me for this. I hope we'll still be friends when this is over." And although I didn't say it aloud, I thought, *And I hope I don't kill you in the meantime.*

I studied the poor spiky face. If I could only get a couple of the ones near his eyes, that would probably buy some time until the doctor arrived.

"Hold still," I whispered. "There's a good boy."

I selected my target, grasped it with

the pliers, said a little prayer, and yanked hard. It came out with a *pop*, and Ajax made a sobbing sound deep in his throat. To my surprise and relief, I held a quill in my instrument.

I held it up to the light to make sure it hadn't broken off. Yes, it was intact. I'd got the whole thing out. I dropped it in a bucket and turned back to Ajax. There was a spot of blood where the quill had been. One down, about three hundred to go. Could I take it? Could my patient?

I found out the answer a few minutes later, and the answer was no. I couldn't bear the terrible noise he made each time, or the blood-tinged drool, or the eyes that were now squeezed completely shut in pain.

A silent tear ran down my face in sympathy with the poor beast. I told myself, buck up, Calpurnia. Do *not* turn into a puddle. You can be a puddle later on but not right now.

Right now you need to

think. All right. This would be so much easier if he wasn't hurting so much. He clearly needs something for his pain (and so do I). I knew that Dr. Pritzker kept a bottle of laudanum to treat animals in pain. I could use that, but how would I get Ajax to drink it?

Could I get it down his throat with a rubber tube? I had seen the doctor use a long, flexible rubber tube to get medicine into a cow. What about an injection? He'd recently bought a newfangled instrument called a hypodermic needle. I'd seen him inject a goat with it. But what was the dose? If you gave an animal too much, you could kill it.

Dr. Pritzker had several books on veterinary medicine, so maybe the answer was in one of those. I pulled a likely one from the shelf and started feverishly paging through it. I was just giving up in frustration when, to my great surprise, Father and Dr. Pritzker burst through the door. The doctor had finished up earlier than expected and they'd met each other on the road.

Dr. Pritzker took one look at Ajax. He might have actually turned a little pale, but he jumped into action, saying, "With that many quills, we'll have to sedate him." I slipped the book back onto the shelf. Father looked from me to the doctor and back again. I figured it was better to try to explain myself later. Dr. Pritzker drew up some laudanum in the hypodermic. He held it up to the light and squinted at the dose and then injected it under the loose skin of Ajax's scruff.

"Let's give him a few minutes to get drowsy before we work on those quills." He cleared his throat and said to my father, "I have to confess, Alfred, I've never seen a dog with so many. There's, uh, some chance that he won't make it. I just want to prepare you."

Ajax slowly sank onto his chest and then his side. He started to snore.

"Ah, good," said the doctor. He took up the pliers.

I handed him the bucket, and he frowned at the handful of quills rattling at the bottom. Uh-oh. Had I done something wrong? Had I somehow broken one off without noticing? Had I condemned Father's favorite dog to a painful end?

"I did it, Dr. Pritzker," I said in a small voice. "I'm sorry."

"No, no, you did fine. Now let's get started on the rest."

Two hours later, the doctor was down to the last handful.

"Calpurnia," Father said, "run for the boys' wagon so we can take him home."

"And bring a blanket," said Dr.

Pritzker, "you'll need to keep him warm until he's back on his feet."

I hobbled out the door and retrieved my boots on the way home. I got back ten minutes later with the wagon and an old horse blanket. Ajax's muzzle and chest were covered in spots and dribbles of blood. I helped Dr. Pritzker clean him up. Father wrapped the limp dog in the blanket and gently lifted him into the wagon.

"Keep him warm tonight," said Dr. Pritzker. "Don't worry about him not eating; it's the drinking that's important at this point. He's not out of the woods yet. I'll come by and check on him in the morning."

Father shook his hand with gratitude. "Doctor, I am forever in your debt."

Father towed our sad burden home in the wagon, and I walked alongside, making sure the blanket didn't slip off. We walked in silence, with many an anxious glance at Ajax on the way. Mother and three of my brothers waited for us at the front door. Father carried the dog into the house and said to my brother Harry, "Ajax is hurt. Dr. Pritzker says we must keep him warm. Build up the fire in the parlor immediately."

Harry stoked the fire, and the flames leaped high. Father put Ajax down on a horse blanket close to the fire. The poor dog had finally achieved his life-long dream of being allowed to sleep inside in front of a roaring fire. But the price he'd paid was far too high.

Everyone ignored me except for Granddaddy, who looked at my blood-streaked clothes and flopping boots.

"Are you hurt?" he said, with such kindness and concern I had to fight back the tears.

"No, Granddaddy," I said. "Ajax found a porcupine. It's dog blood."

"Blood?" said Mother, wheeling around. She took a good look at me and said, "Lamar, stoke the boiler. Calpurnia needs a hot bath."

"Why me?" he pouted.

"Do as I say. Immediately."

He disappeared in a flash. Travis came up to me and said, "Gosh, Callie, what happened to you? You don't look so good."

Suddenly I was overcome with such weariness that I could have fallen asleep right then and there on my feet.

"Straight to bed after your bath, Calpurnia, and don't neglect that hair; it needs a good wash."

I trudged to the bathroom like a sleepwalker.

The next morning, Ajax was still
alive, still asleep by the fire.

Mother let me sleep late, and I
missed breakfast with the family. I ate
in the kitchen with our cook Viola sitting across from me. She gave me the
beady eye and said, "What about this
porcupine, now?"

"It's nothing," I muttered, and stirred my scrambled eggs with my fork.

"A porcupine ain't 'nothing.'"

"Ajax attacked a porcupine, that's all."

"That's the second time in less than a month. I never in my whole life knowed a dog to do that more than one time. One time, and they learn. Generally."

"Yeah, well, he's not the smartest dog in town."

"They say you pulled some of those quills out yourself."

"Yes." I didn't want to talk about it.

I expected a lecture about unladylike

behavior, but she surprised me by saying, "Well, good for you, girl. I had to watch my daddy do that once. It's a hard thing."

She got up, cut a slice of her famous chocolate layer cake, and put it in front of me. "For sure it's a hard thing. For sure."

Her chocolate cake was a rare treat that

was usually saved for special visitors. I perked up a little. Dr. Pritzker arrived, just as I was finishing my slice. I thanked Viola and ran into the parlor, where Father and the doctor and my brothers crowded around Ajax.

The dog's head was swollen to the size of a basketball. He couldn't see, but when he heard Father and felt his hands stroking his flanks, he feebly thumped his tail and tried to lift his head.

"Ah," said Dr. Pritzker, "signs of life." He gently probed the muzzle and jowls with his fingers, looking for any quills he might have missed, or an abscess.

"The problem now will be getting him to drink. He'll need water soon or he'll get dehydrated." The doctor pulled a long, thin rubber tube from his bag. "Calpurnia, bring me a cup of water, or better yet, some beef broth if you have it."

I ran to the kitchen. Viola said there was no beef broth but that she would make some. I drew a small pitcher of water from the kitchen sink pump and took it back to Dr. Pritzker. He attached a funnel to one end of the tube. He said, "Now watch closely. You'll need to give him a small amount of water every hour. Change the water to broth as soon as you can."

He lifted the side of the dog's upper jowl. There was a good-sized gap between the front and back teeth, and he slowly slid the drenching tube through the gap and down the dog's throat. My father and brothers and I stared in fascination. (All except for Travis, who magically disappeared. One minute the boy was there, and the next—*poof!*—he was gone. I never knew how he managed it. But I figured it was better than him sticking around and fainting on us, which was always such a bother.)

Dr. Pritzker said, "Now, Calpurnia, pour half a cup of water slowly into the funnel. Not too fast, or he'll choke. Give it time to go down."

I did as he told me. He then slowly withdrew the tube and handed it to me. "Do you think you can do that every hour?"

"Yessir." It was a good thing it wasn't a school day.

"Well, then." He packed his bag and shook hands with Father, saying, "Don't worry, Alfred, Ajax is in good hands. And I'll check on him again this evening."

Exactly one hour later, my brother Lamar just happened to drift into the parlor as I was preparing the tube. "Careful, now," he sneered, "you don't want to kill Father's favorite dog. Maybe you should let *me* do it."

"What do *you* know about drenching?" I said, doing my best to sneer back. Truthfully, I was a bit nervous, and my rotten brother Lamar wasn't helping things. Poor Ajax. He still looked like a monster. I carefully threaded the tube, which seemed to go down forever, then slowly poured the water into the funnel. The water stayed down, and he didn't gasp or choke. Whew.

I slowly withdrew the tube.

I kept it up all day long. Harry kept the fire stoked high. Ajax slept on. Father seemed worried about this, but Dr. Pritzker had once told me that sleep was Nature's way of healing a sick animal.

By the time the doctor returned that night, I was giving Ajax broth, and it looked to me that maybe—just maybe— the swelling had gone down a bit.

"Well, Calpurnia, I think you're doing a fine job. There's still no sign of abscess or infection. I'm surprised, considering all he's been through."

The next morning, Ajax staggered to his feet, slurped a few mouthfuls of water from his dish, and fell back asleep on his blanket with a thump. He was on the road to recovery. Father was mightily relieved and grateful to both the doctor and me. He gave me a whole quarter for helping out.

My pill of a brother Lamar got in a real huff about that, but my softhearted brother Travis was happy for me.

"Gosh, Callie, what are you going to

do with all that money? Think of all
the penny candy you could buy."

I thought all day about
what I could do with
the money. I finally
bought some toffee at
the general store and
shared it with Travis
(but not Lamar). I
also gave some toffee
to Milly at recess. For
a moment, I thought she was
going to cry, and I couldn't think
why. Then I realized she was a girl who
never got treats like that. A few days

later, she was yanked out of school again, and I didn't see her for a while.

I went to visit her on a Sunday afternoon, the only day of the week I figured she wouldn't have to work in the fields.

Milly was crouched in the yard with a little boy at her side, drawing the ABCs in the dust with a stick. Between them they had no pencils, no copybook, not even a slate to write upon. Both of them were thin and ragged and patched, but it was the lack of a five-cent pencil that especially broke my heart. I, the owner of many pencils, made a vow to fix that.

And as for Ajax? Like I said, some dogs are pretty smart and some dogs are pretty dumb. But even dumb dogs learn in the end, even if they have to learn the hard way. He never went near another porcupine for the rest of his life.